ANIMAL CRACKERS

LONG LIVE ROBERTO

SE IMPEY ★ SHOO RAYNER

ORCHARD BOOKS

ORCHARD BOOKS
338 Euston Road, London NW1 3BH
Orchard Books Australia
Hachette Children's Books
Level 17/207 Kent Street, Sydney NSW 2000

First published by Orchard Books in 1997
This edition published in 2009

Text © Rose Impey 1997
Illustrations © Shoo Rayner 2003

The rights of Rose Impey to be identified as the author and
Shoo Rayner to be identified as the illustrator of this Work
have been asserted by them in accordance with the
Copyright, Designs and Patents Act, 1988.

A CIP catalogue record for this book is available from the British Library.

ISBN 978 1 40830 512 6

1 3 5 7 9 10 8 6 4 2
Printed in China

Orchard Books is a division of Hachette Children's Books,
an Hachette UK company.
www.hachette.co.uk

WREXHAM C.B.C LIBRARY	
LLYFRGELL B.S. WRECSAM	
C56 0000 0485 697	
HJ	25-Nov-2010
JF	£4.99
JFIC	WR

Long Live Roberto

A king could have any pet he wanted:
a gerbil or a giraffe,
a lizard or a llama,
even a lion.
But King Rupert had a rabbit.

The rabbit's name was Roberto.
He wore a gold disc
on the end of a gold chain,
and a little gold crown.
Roberto was a very royal rabbit.

King Rupert ruled over a large
kingdom called Ranga-tanga-roo.
The king had guards to guard him.
He had servants to serve him.
He had advisers to advise him.
And he had lots of friends.

But he had enemies as well.
The king was very rich
and his enemies wanted
to steal his silver and gold
and all his jewels.

King Rupert lived in a tall castle
with a drawbridge.
There were guards at the gates
and on the battlements.
No one could get past the guards.

7

But the king was still afraid.
He was afraid that his enemies
might try to poison him.
Whatever the cook cooked up
King Rupert was afraid to eat it.
Then he got Roberto.

Everywhere the king went,
Roberto went too,
to taste the king's food.

Before the king ate a mouthful,
Roberto tasted it first,
to see if it was poisoned.

Roberto was proud to be the
Royal Food Taster to the king.
From now on King Rupert felt safe.

King Rupert was kind to Roberto.
He gave him a warm bed
to sleep in.

He gave him a throne to sit on.

He even gave him a gold bowl
to eat from.

When the king made a tour of
his kingdom he rode on an elephant.
And so did Roberto.

When the king waved to the people
of Ranga-tanga-roo,
so did Roberto.

And when the people cheered,
"*Long live King Rupert!*"
the king said,
"The people must cheer,
'*Long live Roberto!*' too."

After all, Roberto was
a royal rabbit,
the most royal rabbit in the world.

As the years went by, King Rupert
came to love Roberto more and more.
He loved him better than
his servants and better
than his family and friends.

King Rupert began to worry.
What if anything were to
happen to Roberto?
The king decided to make
his servants taste his food,
before he would let
Roberto taste it.

Just in case it was poisoned.

People began to talk.
They said,"King Rupert loves
that rabbit nearly as much as
he loves himself."
The news spread all round
the kingdom.

King Rupert loves
that rabbit.

Soon the king's enemies heard it.

Two of his enemies were called
Dogbreath and Fleacollar.
They wanted to steal his money.
Fleacollar had an idea:

"Hmmm," said Fleacollar.

The trouble was,
Roberto and the king
went everywhere together.
They even slept in the same room.
The king was guarded day and night,
and so was Roberto.

A week later, the king was travelling through the city.
Suddenly Dogbreath started a fight.

While everyone was busy watching, Fleacollar led Roberto's elephant down a side street,

under a bridge,

along a winding path

and into a secret hideaway.

RANGA TANGA EXPORT Co.

But Roberto was a brave rabbit.
When the kidnappers said,
"Tell us where the king
hides his jewels,"
Roberto wouldn't say a word.

When they said, "Tell us
how to get into the castle,"
his lips were sealed.

And when they told Roberto to put
his paw mark on the ransom note,
brave Roberto refused.

The kidnappers put Roberto
in a cage.
They put the cage in a cellar.
They locked the door
and hid the key.
They left Roberto in the dark,
all on his own.

Then Dogbreath and Fleacollar
sent the ransom note to the king.
It said:

We have Kidnapped
your rabbit.
We want one million
pounds _and_ all your
jewels.

If you do not pay up
we will put him
in a pie.

signed,
Your enemies

The king burst into tears.
He wanted to pay the ransom,
but his advisers said,
"Your Highness, you must never
give money to kidnappers.
Send out the guards,
they'll find Roberto."

The king's guards searched
the whole kingdom.

They took it apart.

They turned it upside down.

They put it back together again.

But they couldn't find Roberto.

The king flew into a temper.
Then his advisers said,
"Your Highness, you must
ask the people for information.
You must offer a reward."
The king's photograph
was in the newspaper.

He was interviewed on TV.

He offered a thousand pounds reward
for the return of the rabbit.

But nobody could find Roberto.

The king took to his bed
and wouldn't speak to anyone.
He gave up all hope
of ever seeing his friend again.

Then one day a little boy
came to the castle.

He told the king that
Dogbreath and Fleacollar
had paid him to find food
for their rabbit.

He showed the guards their secret hideaway.

The guards found Roberto.
They found Dogbreath and
Fleacollar and took them to jail.
They put them in a dark cell,
all on their own.

They took Roberto home
to the castle.

The king was overjoyed.

There was a huge feast
in honour of Roberto,
with a *colossal* cake.

King Rupert and Roberto lived
happily together for many years,
until Roberto died.
One day his heart just stopped.
By then he was a very old rabbit.

The king was sad.
He ordered a huge funeral.
Everyone in the kingdom of
Ranga-tanga-roo came.

Ten thousand people came
to say goodbye to Roberto.
It was the biggest funeral
for a rabbit
there had ever been,
anywhere in the world.
But then, Roberto was a royal rabbit,
the most royal rabbit in the world.

Crack-A-Joke

What's the difference between a rabbit running a race and a rabbit telling jokes?
One's a fit bunny, and the other's a bit funny!

How do you know if carrots are good for you?
When did you last see a rabbit wearing glasses?

Why does a rabbit have a shiny nose?
Because the powder puff is at the wrong end!

Why are rabbits good at maths?
Because they multiply very quickly!

It's a funny bunny business...

How do you hire
a rabbit?
**Put some bricks
under him!**

What do rabbits
play at breaktime?
Hopscotch!

Doctor, Doctor, I keep
thinking I'm a rabbit.

Well hop up
on the couch.

ANIMAL
CRACKERS

COLLECT ALL THE
ANIMAL CRACKERS BOOKS!

All priced at £4.99

Orchard Colour Crunchies are available from all good bookshops, or can be
ordered direct from the publisher:
Orchard Books, PO BOX 29, Douglas IM99 1BQ
Credit card orders please telephone 01624 836000
or fax 01624 837033 or visit our internet site: www.orchardbooks.co.uk
or e-mail: bookshop@enterprise.net for details.
To order please quote title, author and ISBN
and your full name and address.
Cheques and postal orders should be made payable to 'Bookpost plc.'
Postage and packing is FREE within the UK
(overseas customers should add £2.00 per book).
Prices and availability are subject to change.